THE CHRISTMAS SLED

by Carol North
illustrated by Terri Super

MERRIGOLD PRESS • NEW YORK

It is Christmas morning.
Dana and David run downstairs
to see what Santa has left for them.

David finds a tricycle. He is happy. But even happier is Dana when she sees what Santa has left for her. "A sled!" she says. "Oh, it's just what I wanted."

Dana looks at her new sled.
She likes the bright red wood.

David looks at Dana's new sled.
He likes the shiny silvery runners.

Father fixes pancakes for Christmas breakfast. "They taste so good," says Grandma. Dana is the first one to finish eating. "I want to go outside and try my new sled," she says.

Everyone else decides to go outside, too.
They get all bundled up.

Father pulls David and Dana on the sled.
They are going to the big hill.

Grandma and Grandpa and Mother come along.

Dana climbs to the very top of the hill and gets on the sled. "Here I come," she calls out. She whizzes down the hill.

"I want to do that again!" she says.
And she does—two more times.

Then Dana lets David take a turn on the sled.
"Wheeee," he says as the sled flies down the hill.

After a few more rides, the family
starts back to the house.

They stop to watch skaters on the pond.

At home, they build a snowman.

Grandpa adds the final touch
by putting his muffler on the snowman.

David and Dana scoop up snow in a big bowl.
Mother has promised to make snow ice cream.

Inside the warm house, David and Dana
each have a big dish of the ice cream.
"Mmmmm," they say.

At bedtime, Dana says to Father,
"Do you know what? I love my new sled.
It's the best Christmas present I ever got!"